# The Gryphon Press

*—a voice for the voiceless—*

These books are dedicated to those who foster compassion toward all animals.

To my bunny gurus, who are always hopping in to lend a paw:
Meg Brown (fellow volunteer with the Rabbit Resource, the Upstate NY division of the House Rabbit Society),
Evonne Vey (founder of The Natural Rabbit and a marvelous animal artist), Stacie Wogalter (a volunteer
with a bunny barn as big as her heart), and Terra Meierdierck (founder and president
of Bunny and Clyde Rescue). And to all those "bunderful" folks who rescue rabbits.
*—Nancy Furstinger*

To Thea, my young animal-loving friend.
*—Nancy Lane*

Text set in Bernhard Modern by BookMobile Design and Publishing Services
Printed in Canada by Friesens Corporation

Library of Congress Control Number: 2013945366

ISBN: 978-0-940719-19-4

1 3 5 7 9 10 8 6 4 2

A portion of profits from this book will be
donated to shelters and animal rescue societies.

A donation has been made to facilitate the production of this book
in honor of the memory of Norbert N. Bix, a lifelong humanitarian.

*I am the voice of the voiceless:*
*Through me, the dumb shall speak;*
*Till the deaf world's ear be made to hear*
*The cry of the wordless weak.*

*—from a poem by Ella Wheeler Wilcox, early 20th-century poet*

# The Forgotten Rabbit

Written by Nancy Furstinger
Illustrated by Nancy Lane

I wasn't always forgotten.

My mother remembered to give me a daily dose of love.
She shared her love among my eight brothers and sisters.

When we were still babies, the farmer plucked us from our cozy nest.
He drove us to a strange place.

All the children squealed and shrieked when they spotted us.
I huddled together with my brothers and sisters.

A family circled our cage. They poked their fingers
through the wire to stroke my velvety ears.

The children cradled me all the way home.
The boy and the girl giggled when I hopped into a basket
and cracked the colorful eggs.

They called me Bunny. At first, they petted and played with me.
I jumped straight up and wiggled my ears, binkying with joy.

But as spring changed into summer,
they left me in my cage longer and longer.
Some days I never got out.

When my cage started to smell,
they put it in the backyard.
I circled my cage while the
children played and the trees turned
the color of cranberries.

Soon snowflakes frosted my ears and whiskers. My water bottle froze, and I gnawed on the bars of my cage as my stomach rumbled. I curled up tight and tried to disappear.

That night I heard snow crunching. A pair of red boots paused beside my cage. Then gentle hands lifted me out. A girl wrapped me in a warm blanket. She whispered in my ear that the family had given me to her, and that I would never be caged outside again.

The girl laughed as I scampered around my big bunny pen. I periscoped on my back paws to watch while she tossed a sky-high salad.

Soon I had a new name: Bella, which means "beautiful." I also had a new friend: Rosalita. I stopped shaking and shivering when Rosalita stroked my fur.

I stopped quaking and quivering when Rosalita coaxed me out of my
hidey box. She showed me a special surprise: a rabbit jump.

I followed my friend over the jump. Rosalita added more fun equipment
so I could exercise my body and my brain.

One day Rosalita put me in my carrier.
She spoke softly to me during
the car ride. Then we followed signs
to Hoppy Hour, where rabbits
raced around courses.

Soon it was my turn. I zigzagged around poles. I zoomed through tunnels.

I zipped across the teeter-totter. I rocketed up and down a ramp.
I torpedoed through the tire. I hopped over hurdles.

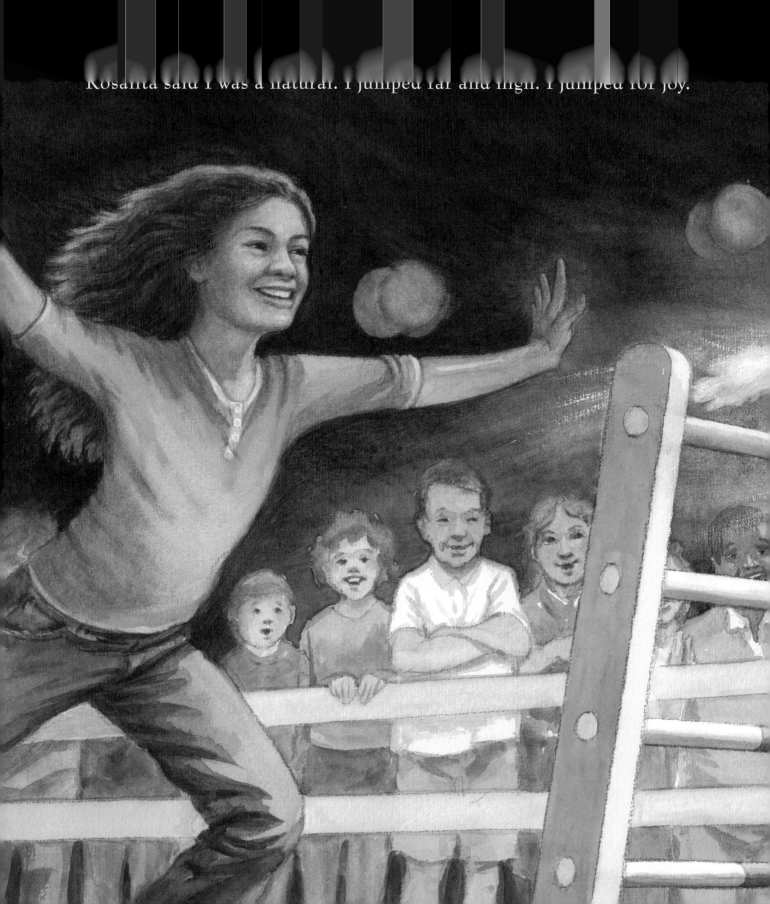

Rosalita said I was a natural. I jumped far and high. I jumped for joy.

I landed on the pause table. The judge gave me a ruby ribbon
that matched my eyes. Rosalita gave me a banana treat.

I chinned Rosalita.
I wanted everyone to know
she was mine.